KEATS

Compiled and Illustrated
by
Patricia Machin

Webb&Bower
EXETER ENGLAND

First published in Great Britain 1985 by
Webb & Bower (Publishers) Limited
9 Colleton Crescent, Exeter, Devon EX2 4BY

Copyright © Webb & Bower (Publishers) Limited 1985

British Library Cataloguing in Publication Data
Keats, John, 1795-1821
  Keats.–(Webb & Bower pocket poets)
  I. Title II. Machin, Patricia
  821'.7 PR4831.5

  ISBN 0-86350-047-1

Typeset in Great Britain by P & M Typesetting Limited,
Exeter, Devon

Printed and bound in Hong Kong by Mandarin Offset
International Limited

Contents

Introduction

John Keats was born on October 31, 1795, in Finsbury, then a village on the outskirts of London; he had two younger brothers and a sister. His father, Thomas Keats, managed livery stables inherited by his wife, Frances. They were a lively ambitious couple with high hopes for the education and future of their children, but Thomas died in a riding accident in 1804 and Frances, having made an unhappy second marriage (through which she lost much of her inheritance) died in December, 1810, and the Keats family future declined. Their maternal grandmother died in 1814 and as she neared the end of her life she chose her neighbour, Richard Abbey, as guardian of her grandchildren because she thought him dependable. She could hardly have made a worse choice: a complete philistine, he had no understanding of the Keats children, caused them great hardship by mis-managing and withholding from them their inheritance and tried totally to repress John's poetical aspirations. In their schooling the boys were much more fortunate. They were educated at Mr. Clarke's school at Enfield where John was a pupil from 1803-11. He was a cheerful mischievous child and grew into a strong, handsome young man (although he was only five feet tall) with a magnetic personality and a brilliant mind which won him, throughout his life, many deep and lasting friendships. It was not until his mother died that he became studious and started to read voraciously. Cowden Clarke, son of the headmaster, guided and encouraged him and became a life-long friend. In October, 1815, Keats entered Guy's Hospital and the following year passed the examination that would allow him to practise an an apothercary and surgeon but he decided that his vocation was to write poetry.

A landmark in his life was the emigration to America of his brother George and the tragic death from consumption of Tom, his youngest brother. It is believed that Keats himself contracted the disease from nursing Tom for he was soon to suffer the symptoms. His love letters are evidence of the passionate feeling he had for the young girl, Fanny Brawne, a romance that did not run smoothly, due possibly to her temperament as well as to Keats' poverty. When he felt that he had not long to live he released her from her engagement to him and on the insistence of his friends went to Italy for the winter in an attempt to recover. He died there on February 23, 1821.

This poem is believed to have been written at the time when Keats was apprenticed to the surgeon Hammond close to the house in Edmonton where the Keats children lived with their grandmother. After her death the house, which had been home to the children for nearly nine years, was closed and George and Tom were sent to work at their guardian's counting-house. Perhaps because of his loneliness, Keats at this period began to spend more time writing poetry.

Song

STAY, ruby-breasted warbler, stay,
  And let me see thy sparkling eye,
Oh brush not yet the pearl-strung spray
  Nor bow thy pretty head to fly.

Stay while I tell thee, fluttering thing,
  That thou of love an emblem art,
Yes! patient plume thy little wing,
  Whilst I my thoughts to thee impart.

When summer nights the dews bestow,
  And summer suns enrich the day,
Thy notes the blossoms charm to blow,
  Each opes delighted at thy lay.

So when in youth the eye's dark glance
  Speaks pleasure from its circle bright,
The tones of love our joys enhance
  And make superior each delight.

And when bleak storms resistless rove,
  And every rural bliss destroy,
Nought comforts then the leafless grove
  But thy soft note—its only joy—

E'en so the words of love beguile
  When Pleasure's tree no flower bears,
And draw a soft endearing smile
  Amid the gloom of grief and tears.

Since he was homeless in the autumn of 1816, Keats took lodgings near Guy's Hospital although he had finished his training there in July. This area of London, then called The Borough, was well known for its prisons, hospitals and crowded tenements, the haunt of London's underworld. Keats wrote that it was 'a beastly place in dirt turnings and windings' and these two sonnets reflect his feelings when contrasting it with the countryside he had left.

Happy is England! I could be content
  To see no other verdure than its own;
  To feel no other breezes than are blown
Through its tall woods with high romances blent:
Yet do I sometimes feel a languishment
  For skies Italian, and an inward groan
  To sit upon an Alp as on a throne,
And half forget what world or worldling meant.
Happy is England, sweet her artless daughters;
  Enough their simple loveliness for me,
    Enough their whitest arms in silence clinging;
  Yet do I often warmly burn to see
    Beauties of deeper glance, and hear their singing,
And float with them about the summer waters.

To one who has been long in city pent,
  'Tis very sweet to look into the fair
    And open face of to heaven,—to breathe
               a prayer
Full in the smile of the blue firmament.
Who is more happy, when, with heart's
               content,
  Fatigued he sinks into some pleasant lair
  Of wavy grass, and reads a debonair
And gentle tale of love and languishment?
Returning home at evening, with an ear
  Catching the notes of Philomel,—an eye
Watching the sailing cloudlet's bright career,
  He mourns that day so soon has glided by:
E'en like the passage of an angel's tear
  That falls through the clear ether silently.

O SOLITUDE! if I must with thee dwell,
  Let it not be among the jumbled heap
  Of murky buildings; climb with me the steep,—
Nature's observatory—whence the dell,
It's flowery slopes, its river's crystal swell,
  May seem a span; let me thy vigils keep
    'Mongst boughs pavillion'd, where the deer's
                                    swift leap
Startles the wild bee from the fox-glove bell.
But though I'll gladly trace these scenes with thee,
  Yet the sweet converse of an innocent mind,
  Whose words are images of thoughts refin'd,
Is my soul's pleasure; and it sure must be
  Almost the highest bliss of human-kind,
When to thy haunts two kindred spirits flee.

While Keats was in lodgings in The Borough in 1816 he had a memorable reunion in October with his former schoolfriend, Cowden Clarke, now living in London. Together they read Clarke's folio copy of Chapman's 'Homer' until daybreak, after which Keats walked the two miles back to his lodgings and wrote this masterpiece in time for Clarke to find it on his breakfast table a few hours later.

On First Looking into
Chapman's Homer

MUCH have I travell'd in the realms of gold,
    And many goodly states and kingdoms seen;
    Round many western islands have I been
Which bards in fealty to Apollo hold.
Oft of one wide expanse had I been told
    That deep-brow'd Homer ruled as his demesne;
    Yet did I never breathe its pure serene
Till I heard Chapman speak out loud and bold:
Then felt I like some watcher of the skies
    When a new planet swims into his ken;
Or like stout Cortez when with eagle eyes
    He star'd at the Pacific—and all his men
Look'd at each other with a wild surmise—
    Silent, upon a peak in Darien.

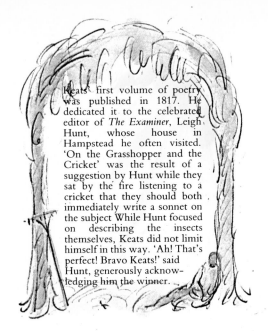

Keats' first volume of poetry was published in 1817. He dedicated it to the celebrated editor of *The Examiner*, Leigh Hunt, whose house in Hampstead he often visited. 'On the Grasshopper and the Cricket' was the result of a suggestion by Hunt while they sat by the fire listening to a cricket that they should both immediately write a sonnet on the subject While Hunt focused on describing the insects themselves, Keats did not limit himself in this way. 'Ah! That's perfect! Bravo Keats!' said Hunt, generously acknowledging him the winner.

On the Grasshopper and Cricket

THE poetry of earth is never dead:
  When all the birds are faint with the hot sun,
  And hide in cooling trees, a voice will run
From hedge to hedge about the new-mown mead;
That is the Grasshopper's—he takes the lead
  In summer luxury,—he has never done
  With his delights; for when tired out with fun
He rests at ease beneath some pleasant weed.
The poetry of earth is ceasing never:
  On a lone winter evening, when the frost
    Has wrought a silence, from the stove there shrills
The Cricket's song, in warmth increasing ever,
  And seems to one in drowsiness half lost,
    The Grasshopper's among some grassy hills.

Keats wrote this poem about five days after the death of his grandmother, Mrs. Jennings, a tragic loss to the Keats children. Years later he disclosed to a friend, Richard Woodhouse, that he had told no one at the time, not even his own brothers with whom he was on very close terms. Woodhouse had unfailing faith in Keats, lending him one from time to time which he tactfully pretended was an advance from the publishers.

On Death

CAN death be sleep, when life is but a dream,
  And scenes of bliss pass as a phantom by?
The transient pleasures as a vision seem,
  And yet we think the greatest pain's to die.

How strange it is that man on earth should roam,
  And lead a life of woe, but not forsake
His rugged path; nor dare he view alone
  His future doom which is but to awake.

In writing the 4000 lines which comprise the poem *Endymion*, the self-taught Keats was committing himself to acquire experience in the full knowledge (as he writes in the preface to the poem) of his shortcomings and inadequacy. Based on Greek mythology, although the allegory is somewhat obscure, the poem contains beautiful passages and is generally considered the work of an immature genius. The twenty-five lines that open the poem are given here.

Lines from Endymion

A THING of beauty is a joy for ever:
Its loveliness increases; it will never
Pass into nothingness; but still will keep
A bower quiet for us, and a sleep
Full of sweet dreams, and health, and quiet breathing.
Therefore, on every morrow, are we wreathing
A flowery band to bind us to the earth,
Spite of despondence, of the inhuman dearth
Of noble natures, of the gloomy days,
Of all the unhealthy and o'er-darkened ways
Made for our searching: yes, in spite of all,
Some shape of beauty moves away the pall
From our dark spirits. Such the sun, the moon,
Trees old, and young, sprouting a shady boon
For simple sheep; and such are daffodils
With the green world they live in; and clear rills
That for themselves a cooling covert make
'Gainst the hot season; the mid forest brake,
Rich with a sprinkling of fair musk-rose blooms:
And such too is the grandeur of the dooms
We have imagined for the mighty dead;
All lovely tales that we have heard or read;
An endless fountain of immortal drink,
Pouring unto us from the heaven's brink.

Keats met John Hamilton Reynolds in October, 1816. Although only a year older than Keats, Reynolds was an established writer and a brilliant and amusing companion. The poet was made welcome by his parents and four sisters at their home in Conduit Street. This must have been some compensation to Keats who felt so strongly the lack of family life. He wrote several poems to amuse the girls, including this sonnet which was published posthumously.

On Mrs Reynolds's Cat

CAT! who hast pass'd thy grand climacteric,
  How many mice and rats hast in thy days
  Destroye'd?—How many tit bits stolen? Gaze
With those bright languid segments green, and prick
Those velvet ears—but pr'ythee do not stick
  Thy latent talons in me—and upraise
  Thy gentle mew—and tell me all thy frays
Of fish and mice, and rats and tender chick.
Nay, look not down, nor lick thy dainty wrists—
  For all the wheezy asthma,— and for all
Thy tail's tip is nick'd off—and though the fists
  Of many a maid have given thee many a maul,
Still is that fur as soft as when the lists
  In youth thou enter'dst on glass-bottled wall.

Keats considered that his poem 'Bards of Passion' carried on from 'Lines on the Mermaid Tavern' except that the theme now, he explained in a letter to his brother George, is the double immortality of the poets in that their souls on earth are speaking to us and sustaining us through their poetry. Keats liked the brisk metre of these poems and found them a stimulating contrast to sonnet writing.

Lines on the Mermaid Tavern

SOULS of Poets dead and gone,
What Elysium have ye known,
Happy field or mossy cavern,
Choicer than the Mermaid Tavern?
Have ye tippled drink more fine
Than mine host's Canary wine?
Or are fruits of Paradise
Sweeter than those dainty pies
Of venison? O generous food!
Drest as though bold Robin Hood
Would, with his maid Marian,
Sup and bowse from horn and can.

I have heard that on a day
Mine host's sign-board flew away,
Nobody knew whither, till
An astrologer's old quill
To a sheepskin gave the story,
Said he saw you in your glory,
Underneath a new old sign
Sipping beverage divine,
And pledging with contented smack
The Mermaid in the Zodiac.
Souls of Poets dead and gone,
What Elysium have ye known,
Happy field or mossy cavern,
Choicer than the Mermaid Tavern?

BARDS of Passion and of Mirth,
Ye have left your souls on earth!
Have ye souls in heaven too,
Double lived in regions new?
Yes, and those of heaven commune
With the spheres of sun and moon;
With the noise of fountains wond'rous,
And the parle of voices thund'rous;
With the whisper of heaven's trees
And one another, in soft ease
Seated on Elysian lawns
Brows'd by none but Dian's fawns;
Underneath large blue-bells tented,
Where the daisies are rose-scented,
And the rose herself has got
Perfume which on earth is not;
Where the nightingale doth sing
Not a senseless, tranced thing,
But divine melodious truth;
Philosophic numbers smooth;
Tales and golden histories
Of heaven and its mysteries.

Thus ye live on high, and then
On the earth ye live again;
And the souls ye left behind you
Teach us, here, the way to find you,
Where your other souls are joying,
Never slumber'd, never cloying.
Here, your earth-born souls still speak
To mortals, of their little week;
Of their sorrows and delights;
Of their passions and their spites;
Of their glory and their shame;
What doth strengthen and what maim.
Thus ye teach us, every day,
Wisdom, though fled far away.

Bards of Passion and of Mirth,
Ye have left your souls on earth!
Ye have souls in heaven too,
Double-lived in regions new!

During the winter of 1818-19 when Keats was wrestling with his long and testing poem *Hyperion* he sought relief by writing some verse in the spirit of the seventeenth century. The poem 'Fancy' contains a potentially serious theme developed later in the Odes but it has a sprightly metre. It was at this time, and for the same reason, Keats wrote 'I had a Dove' which he described as 'a little thing I wrote off to some music as it was playing'.

I HAD a dove and the sweet dove died;
  And I have thought it died of grieving:
O, what could it grieve for? Its feet were tied,
  With a silken thread of my own hand's weaving;
Sweet little red feet! why should you die—
Why should you leave me, sweet dove! why?
You liv'd alone on the forest-tree,
Why, pretty thing! could you not live with me?
I kiss'd you oft and gave you white peas;
Why not live sweetly, as in the green trees?

EVER let the fancy roam,
Pleasure never is at home:
At a touch sweet Pleasure melteth,
Like to bubbles when rain pelteth;
Then let winged Fancy wander
Through the thought still spread beyond her:
Open wide the mind's cage-door,
She'll dart forth, and cloudward soar.
O sweet Fancy! let her loose;
Summer's joys are spoilt by use,
And the enjoying of the Spring
Fades as does its blossoming;
Autumn's red-lipp'd fruitage too,
Blushing through the mist and dew,
Cloys with tasting: What do then?
Sit thee by the ingle, when
The sear faggot blazes bright,
Spirit of a winter's night;
When the soundless earth is muffled,
And the caked snow is shuffled
From the ploughboy's heavy shoon;
When the Night doth meet the Noon
In a dark conspiracy
To banish Even from her sky.

Sit thee there, and send abroad,
With a mind self-overaw'd,
Fancy, high-commission'd:—send her!
She has vassals to attend her:
She will bring, in spite of frost,
Beauties that the earth hath lost;
She will bring thee, all together,
All delights of summer weather;
All the buds and bells of May,
From dewy sward or thorny spray;
All the heaped Autumn's wealth,
With a still, mysterious stealth:
She will mix these pleasures up
Like three fit wines in a cup,
And thou shalt quaff it:—thou shalt hear
Distant harvest-carols clear;
Rustle of the reaped corn;
Sweet birds antheming the morn:
And, in the same moment—hark!
'Tis the early April lark,
Or the rooks, with busy caw,
Foraging for sticks and straw.
Thou shalt, at one glance, behold
The daisy and the marigold;

White-plum'd lillies, and the first
Hedge-grown primrose that hath burst;
Shaded hyacinth, alway
Sapphire queen of the mid-May;
And every leaf, and every flower
Pearled with the self-same shower.
Thou shalt see the field-mouse peep
Meagre from its celled sleep;
And the snake all winter-thin
Cast on sunny bank its skin;
Freckled nest-eggs thou shalt see
Hatching in the hawthorn-tree,
When the hen-bird's wing doth rest
Quiet on her mossy nest;
Then the hurry and alarm
When the bee-hive casts its swarm;
Acorns ripe down-pattering,
While the autumn breezes sing.

Oh, sweet Fancy! let her loose;
Every thing is spoilt by use:
Where's the cheek that doth not fade,
Too much gaz'd at? Where's the maid
Whose lip mature is ever new?

Where's the eye, however blue,
Doth not weary? Where's the face
One would meet in every place?
Where's the voice, however soft,
One would hear so very oft?
At a touch sweet Pleasure melteth
Like to bubbles when rain pelteth.
Let, then, winged Fancy find
Thee a mistress to thy mind:
Dulcet-eyed as Ceres' daughter,
Ere the God of Torment taught her
How to frown and how to chide;
With a waist and with a side
White as Hebe's, when her zone
Slipt its golden clasp, and down
Fell her kirtle to her feet,
While she held the goblet sweet,
And Jove grew languid.—Break the mesh
Of the Fancy's silken leash;
Quickly break her prison-string
And such joys as these she'll bring.—
Let the winged Fancy roam,
Pleasure never is at home.

To finish his long poem *Endymion* Keats went to stay at Burford Bridge near Dorking. After completing it he did not immediately return to Hampstead where he was living with his brothers. The trees near the inn where he was staying were now bare and he compared the imperviousness of nature to the pain of regret and memories that human beings have to suffer in this poem, which he wrote before returning home in December, 1817, with his completed *Endymion*.

In drear-nighted December,
    Too happy, happy tree,
Thy Branches ne'er remember
    Their green felicity:
The north cannot undo them,
With a sleety whistle through them;
Nor frozen thawings glue them
    From budding at the prime.

In drear-nighted December,
    Too happy, happy Brook,
Thy bubblings ne'er remember
    Apollo's summer look;
But with a sweet forgetting,
They stay their crystal fretting,
Never, never petting
    About the frozen time.

Ah! would 'twere so with many
    A gentle girl and boy!
But were there ever any
    Writh'd not of passed joy?
The feel of not to feel it,
When there is none to heal it,
Nor numbed sense to steel it,
    Was never said in rhyme.

In the spring of 1819 Keats wrote, within a month, the miraculous Odes for which he is best remembered. After the tragedy of his brother Tom's death, his dependable and generous friend Charles Brown arranged for him to share his house in Hampstead. This ballad was written just before the Odes. It was composed on the afternoon of April 21 and in the evening he included it in his journal-letter to his brother George.

La Belle Dame Sans Merci

O, what can ail thee, knight-at-arms,
　　Alone and palely loitering?
The sedge has wither'd from the lake,
　　And no birds sing.

O, what can ail thee, knight-at-arms,
　　So haggard and so woe-begone?
The squirrel's granary is full,
　　And the harvest's done.

I see a lilly on thy brow,
　　With anguish moist and fever dew;
And on thy cheeks a fading rose
　　Fast withereth too.

I met a lady in the meads,
　　Full beautiful—a faery's child,
Her hair was long, her foot was light,
　　And her eyes were wild.

I made a garland for her head,
    And bracelets too, and fragrant zone;
She look'd at me as she did love,
    And made sweet moan.

I set her on my pacing steed,
    And nothing else saw all day long;
For sidelong would she bend, and sing
    A faery's song.

She found me roots of relish sweet,
    And honey wild, and manna dew,
And sure in language strange she said—
    'I love thee true'.

She took me to her elfin grot,
    And there she wept and sigh'd full sore,
And there I shut her wild wild eyes
    With kisses four.

And there she lulled me asleep
   And there I dream'd—Ah! woe betide!
The latest dream I ever dream'd
   On the cold hill side.

I saw pale kings and princes too,
   Pale warriors, death-pale were they all;
They cried—'La Belle Dame sans Merci
   Hath thee in thrall!'

I saw their starved lips in the gloam,
   With horrid warning gaped wide,
And I awoke and found me here,
   On the cold hill's side.

And this is why I sojourn here
   Alone and palely loitering,
Though the sedge has wither'd from the lake,
   And no birds sing.

One of the greatest English lyrics, this Ode was written in two or three hours. Charles Brown writes: 'In the spring of 1819 a nightingale had built her nest near my house. Keats felt a tranquil and continual joy in her song; and one morning he took his chair from the breakfast-table to the grass-plot under a plum-tree, where he sat for two or three hours. When he came into the house, I perceived he had some scraps of paper in his hand, and these he was quietly thrusting behind the books. On inquiry, I found those scraps, four or five in number, contained his poetic feeling on the song of our nightingale.'

Ode to a Nightingale

My heart aches, and a drowsy numbness pains
   My sense, as though of hemlock I had drunk,
Or emptied some dull opiate to the drains
   One minute past, and Lethe-wards had sunk:
'Tis not through envy of thy happy lot,
   But being too happy in thine happiness,—
      That thou, light-winged Dryad of the trees,
        In some melodious plot
Of beechen green, and shadows numberless,
   Singest of summer in full-throated ease.

O, for a draught of vintage! that hath been
   Cool'd a long age in the deep-delved earth,
Tasting of Flora and the country green,
   Dance, and Provencal song, and sunburnt mirth!
O for a beaker full of the warm South,
   Full of the true, the blushful Hippocrene,
      With beaded bubbles winking at the brim,
        And purple-stained mouth;
That I might drink, and leave the world unseen,
   And with thee fade away into the forest dim:

Fade far away, dissolve, and quite forget
    What thou among the leaves hast never known,
The weariness, the fever, and the fret
    Here, where men sit and hear each other groan;
Where palsy shakes a few, sad, last gray hairs,
    Where youth grows pale, and spectre-thin, and dies;
        Where but to think is to be full of sorrow
            And leaden-eyed despairs,
        Where Beauty cannot keep her lustrous eyes,
            Or new Love pine at them beyond to-morrow.

Away! away! for I will fly to thee,
    Not charioted by Bacchus and his pards,
But on the viewless wings of Poesy,
    Though the dull brain perplexes and retards:
Already with thee! tender is the night,
    And haply the Queen-Moon is on her throne,
        Cluster'd around by all her starry Fays;
            But here there is no light,
        Save what from heaven is with the breezes blown
            Through verdurous glooms and winding mossy ways.

I cannot see what flowers are at my feet,
    Nor what soft incense hangs upon the boughs,
But, in embalmed darkness, guess each sweet
    Wherewith the seasonable month endows
The grass, the thicket, and the fruit-tree wild;
    White hawthorn, and the pastoral eglantine;
        Fast fading violets cover'd up in leaves;
            And mid-May's eldest child,
        The coming musk-rose, full of dewy wine,
            The murmurous haunt of flies on summer eves.

Darkling I listen; and, for many a time
    I have been half in love with easeful Death,
Call'd him soft names in many a mused rhyme,
    To take into the air my quiet breath;
Now more than ever seems it rich to die,
    To cease upon the midnight with no pain,
        While thou art pouring forth thy soul abroad
            In such an ecstasy!
Still wouldst thou sing, and I have ears in vain—
    To thy high requiem become a sod.

Thou wast not born for death, immortal Bird!
    No hungry generations tread thee down;
The voice I hear this passing night was heard
    In ancient days by emperor and clown:
Perhaps the self-same song that found a path
    Through the sad heart of Ruth, when, sick for home,
        She stood in tears amid the alien corn;
            The same that oft-times hath
Charm'd magic casements, opening on the foam
    Of perilous seas, in faery lands forlorn.

Forlorn! the very word is like a bell
    To toll me back from thee to my sole self!
Adieu! the fancy cannot cheat so well
    As she is fam'd to do, deceiving elf.
Adieu! adieu! thy plaintive anthem fades
    Past the near meadows, over the still stream,
        Up the hill-side; and now 'tis buried deep
            In the next valley glades:
Was it a vision, or a waking dream?
    Fled is that music:—Do I wake or sleep?

Keats' letters to his family and friends are among the greatest collections in English Literature. In them he displays dazzling qualities of which he is the complete master. 'My dear Reynolds' he concludes in a letter to his friend on January 31, 1818, 'you must forgive all this ranting – but the fact is I cannot write sense this Morning – however you shall have some – I will copy my last sonnet.' There followed this moving poem, perhaps containing a premonition of his own untimely death.

WHEN I have fears that I may cease to be
   Before my pen has glean'd my teeming brain,
Before, high piled books, in charactery,
   Hold like rich garners the full ripen'd grain;
When I behold, upon the night's starr'd face,
   Huge cloudy symbols of a high romance,
And think that I may never live to trace
   Their shadows, with the magic hand of chance;
And when I feel, fair creature of an hour,
   That I shall never look upon thee more,
Never have relish in the faery power
   Of unreflecting love;—then on the shore
Of the wide world I stand alone, and think
Till love and fame to nothingness do sink.

This is the last of the great Odes of Keats, written in the autumn following his brilliant output in the spring of 1819, when he was staying in Canterbury. 'To Autumn' is considered one of the most perfect poems in the English language. Its timeless evocative power cannot fail to stir the imagination of generations of readers.

To Autumn

SEASON of mists and mellow fruitfulness,
  Close bosom-friend of the maturing sun;
Conspiring with him how to load and bless
  With fruit the vines that round the thatch-eves run;
To bend with apples the moss'd cottage-trees,
  And fill all fruit with ripeness to the core;
    To swell the gourd, and plump the hazel shells
  With a sweet kernel; to set budding more,
And still more, later flowers for the bees,
Until they think warm days will never cease,
    For Summer has o'er-brimm'd their
              clammy cells.

Who hath not seen thee oft amid thy store?
  Sometimes whoever seeks abroad may find
Thee sitting careless on a granary floor,
  Thy hair soft-lifted by the winnowing wind;
Or on a half-reap'd furrow sound asleep,
  Drows'd with the fume of poppies, while thy hook
  Spares the next swath and all its twined flowers:
And sometimes like a gleaner thou dost keep
  Steady thy laden head across a brook;
  Or by a cyder-press, with patient look,
    Thou watchest the last oozings hours by hours.

Where are the songs of Spring? Ay, where are they?
  Think not of them, thou has thy music too,—
While barred clouds bloom the soft-dying day,
  And touch the stubble-plains with rosy hue;
Then in a wailful choir the small gnats mourn
  Among the river sallows, borne aloft
    Or sinking as the light wind lives or dies;
And full-grown lambs loud bleat from hilly bourn;
  Hedge-crickets sing; and now with treble soft
  The red-breast whistles from a garden-croft;
    And gathering swallows twitter in the skies.